How Mrs Monkey Missed The Ark

Judith Kerr

PictureLions

An Imprint of HarperCollins*Publishers*

For my family, with love

First published in Great Britain by
HarperCollins Publishers Ltd in 1992
First published in Picture Lions in 1993
Picture Lions is an imprint of the Children's Division,
part of HarperCollins Publishers Limited,
77-85 Fulham Palace Road, Hammersmith,
London W6 8JB

Text and illustrations copyright © Judith Kerr 1992

The author/illustrator asserts the moral right to be
identified as the author/illustrator of the work.

ISBN: 0 00 664149-0

Printed in Great Britain

This book is set in 16/19 Goudy

One day long, long ago God said to Noah,
"It's going to rain. It's going to rain a lot and for a long time.
You'd better build an ark."
"What's an ark?" said Noah.
"A big boat," said God. "You'll need it to save the animals
when the rain starts."
So Noah built the ark and Mrs Noah helped.

It turned out quite well in the end.

"Now you must call the animals," said God.
"There will be two of each kind."
So Noah called the animals, and they all
came and stood and looked at each other
and wondered what would happen next.
And just then it started to rain.
"See?" said God.

"Time to go," said Noah.
"Time to go," said Mr and Mrs Giraffe.

"Time to go," said Mr and Mrs Elephant.
"Time to go," said Mr Monkey.
But Mrs Monkey said, "I just want to
get a little fruit to eat on the journey.
You go ahead and I'll catch you up."

She ran back into the jungle and up and up and up and up and up to the top of a very tall tree.

"Now what would be nice?"
said Mrs Monkey.
"A nice mixture, I think.
Bananas and oranges and
dates and figs and..."

But by now it was raining so hard that Mrs Monkey had to stop thinking and make herself an umbrella instead. This took quite a long time.

Then she found some bananas. But some were too big, and some were too small, and some were too ripe, and some were not ripe enough. So this, too, took a long time.

The dates took even longer because Mrs Monkey had to keep tasting them to see if they were nice enough. And after this she could find no other fruit at all.

At last after a very, very long time she said,
"Well, I don't call this a nice mixture.
But I'd better go back to the ark."
But when she looked down she had a big surprise. There was
water everywhere. It was way up the tree and rising fast.

There was water everywhere round the ark too.
It was floating far away.
"Where's Mrs Monkey?" said Noah.
"She's going to catch us up," said Mr Monkey.
"We can't see her," said Mr and Mrs Giraffe.

But just then
God saw her.
"Dear Me," said God.
"What's Mrs Monkey
doing in that tree?
She should be
on the ark.
I'd better send her
something that can swim."

"A dolphin. That's nice," said Mrs Monkey.
"I never knew they lived in the tree tops.
Perhaps it will take me to the ark."

"Jumping about
all over the water
won't get us there,"
said Mrs Monkey
a little later.

"I don't think this dolphin wants to go to the ark," said Mrs Monkey later still.

"Mr Monkey will wonder where I am," said Mrs Monkey. "And I haven't even got him a nice fruity mixture to eat."

Then she saw something.

"Stop!" shouted Mrs Monkey. "Oranges!" shouted Mrs Monkey.

Mrs Monkey picked all she wanted.
"Bananas, dates and oranges," she said. "That's very nearly a
nice mixture, and I can ride on this branch instead of the dolphin."

The birds were very surprised. The fish were surprised too.

But Mrs Monkey was heavier than the birds,
and a big storm was blowing up.

A big storm was blowing round the ark too.
"Are you sure Mrs Monkey is catching us up?" said Noah.
"Quite sure," said Mr Monkey.
"But where is she?" said Mr and Mrs Giraffe.

Mrs Monkey was under the water.
It was very quiet under the water.
The trees hardly moved.
Fish flew through their
branches instead of birds.

They were finding
new things
to eat.
The fish were
eating figs.

They were the nicest, ripest figs
Mrs Monkey had ever seen, and
there were plenty for everyone.
"Bananas, oranges, dates and figs,"
said Mrs Monkey. "I always knew
I'd find a nice mixture in the end."

But when she swam back to the top of the water the branch
had gone and the dolphin had gone. It was blowing harder
than ever and there were big waves everywhere.

God was trying to peer through the storm.
He thought He could see something in the water.
"Stop!" said God, and the storm stopped. "Just as I thought,"
said God. "It's Mrs Monkey. *Now* what's happened to her?
I'd better send her something that can fly."

"What a nice clean bird," said Mrs Monkey. "Perhaps flying will dry my fur. And I do believe it's raining less at last."

The bird flew through the rain and through the clouds
to the sunshine above.

The sun dried Mrs Monkey's fur. It dried the fruit and it dried the bird.

It flew and flew and flew.

They flew for days and days until at last they came to a hole in the clouds.

Mrs Monkey peered through it. Then she shouted, "Wait! It's stopped raining! I can see land and I can see the ark!"

The ark had landed on top of a mountain. Mrs Monkey decided to land as well.

"Here I come!" she shouted. "And look what I've got!

Bananas and dates
and oranges and figs!

A really nice mixture!"

"I told you Mrs Monkey would catch us up," said Mr Monkey.

But when they looked, Mrs Monkey's
fruit was no longer nice.
The sun had dried it all up.
There was nothing left but
dried up skin and pips.
"Oh dear," said Mrs Monkey.

And then a very surprising thing happened.
The pips all came together into one big pip.

And that pip grew...

and grew...

and grew.

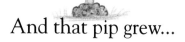

It grew into a big tree. It was a tree no one had ever seen. It was a tree with oranges and figs and bananas and dates all growing together on its branches. "They make a nice mixture," said God.

"And another thing," said God. "All this water has been a lot of trouble. I'm going to make sure it never rains like that again."